Come
Here,
Cat

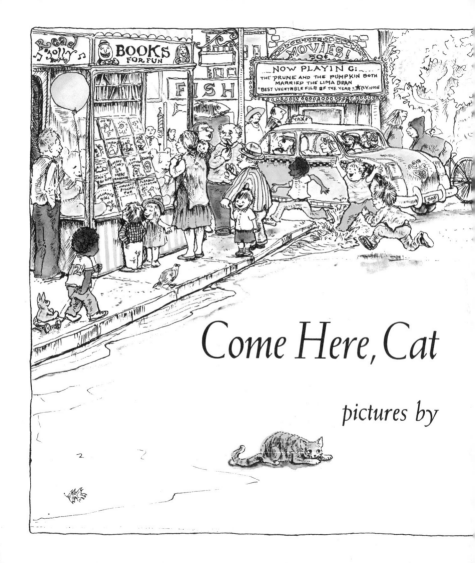

Come Here, Cat

pictures by

Joan Lexan Nødset

by Joan L. Nødset

Steven Kellogg

HarperCollins*Publishers*

For Tiger Lexau, Midnight Holliday,
Lilliput Dicks, and most of all
for that Ptolemy Kayden
—JLN

To Secondhand Rose, Madame Butterfly,
Dr. Pepper, and Lola Bird
—SK

COME HERE, CAT
Text copyright © 1973 by Joan L. Nødset
Pictures copyright © 1973 by Steven Kellogg
Printed in the U.S.A. All rights reserved.
Library of Congress Catalog Card Number 92-39005
ISBN 0-06-024557-3
ISBN 0-06-024558-1 (lib. bdg.)

Come here, cat.
Come here, you pretty cat.
I like you, cat.

Why don't you come?
Don't you like me?

Then I'll come to you, cat.

You don't like me
to carry you that way?
I'm sorry, cat.

I won't do it again.
Please don't be mad.

Can I pet you, cat?

Oh, you nice soft cat!

I didn't mean to pull your tail.
You ran away
when I was petting it.

Did I hurt you, cat?

Oh, I hurt your feelings.
I'm sorry, cat.
I didn't mean to.

I'll put you on my lap.

Stay here, now.

That's a good cat.

Yes, you can lick my face.
That feels funny.
Your tongue feels so rough.

I like you too, cat.

Don't bite me, cat.

Don't, don't, don't!

Bad cat!

Oh, you were playing.

Well, you scared me, cat.

That's why I pushed you.

But it's okay now.
You can come back, cat.

Did I scare you too?
Look, I'll sit here,
nice and quiet.

Closer, cat.

Closer, closer.

That's it.

Just a little more.

I love you, cat!

Oh, cat!
I hear your motor.